THE JUPITER TWINS

FIELD TRIP TO MARS

BY JEFF DINARDO
ILLUSTRATED BY DAVE CLEGG

RED
CHAIR
•PRESS•

Funny Bone Books

and Funny Bone Readers are produced and published by

Red Chair Press LLC   PO Box 333   South Egremont, MA 01258-0333

www.redchairpress.com

About the Author

Jeff Dinardo's books are filled with humor and silliness that captures a child's imagination. When not writing, Jeff runs a successful design firm specializing in textbooks for use in classrooms from K-8.

About the Artist

Dave Clegg lives and works on a small horse farm in north Georgia with his wife Lyn. All of Dave's work is done digitally on his computer. When he is not drawing, he can be found creating songs with his guitar or making robot sculptures!

Publisher's Cataloging-In-Publication Data
Names: Dinardo, Jeffrey. | Clegg, Dave, illustrator.
Title: The Jupiter twins. Book 1, Field trip to Mars / by Jeff Dinardo ; illustrated by Dave Clegg.
Other Titles: Field trip to Mars

Description: South Egremont, MA : Red Chair Press, [2018] | Series: Funny bone books. First
    chapters | Interest age level: 005-007. | Summary: "Trudy and Tina are best friends. They
    are also twins. Trudy loves adventure and Tina is happy to go along for the ride--as long as
    it is a smooth ride! Today the class is going on a field trip to Mars. Enjoy the fun on the Red
    Planet. First Chapters books are easy introductions to exploring longer text."--Provided by
    publisher.

Identifiers: LCCN 2017934021 | ISBN 978-1-63440-249-1 (library hardcover)
    | ISBN 978-1-63440-253-8 (paperback) | ISBN 978-1-63440-257-6 (ebook)

Subjects: LCSH: Twins--Juvenile fiction. | Mars (Planet)--Juvenile fiction. | Outer space--
    Exploration--Juvenile fiction. | School field trips--Juvenile fiction. | CYAC: Twins--Fiction.
    | Mars (Planet)--Fiction. | Outer space--Exploration--Fiction. | School field trips--Fiction.

Classification: LCC PZ7.D6115 Juf 2018 (print) | LCC PZ7.D6115 (ebook) | DDC [E]--dc23

Printed in Canada

0118 2P FRNS18

CONTENTS

Meet the Characters

Trudy

Tina

Ms. Bickleblorb

Spot

All the kids got off the space bus.

"Please stay with your partners," said their teacher, Ms. Bickleblorb. "Have fun exploring Mars. But be careful!" she added.

Trudy and Tina were partners, as always.

They were also twins.

"Bored!" yawned Trudy as she kicked a Mars rock with her foot.

"I hope it doesn't rain," said Tina.

Some students went to collect rocks. Others went to hike a nearby mountain. Trudy and Tina just sat on the red dirt.

Trudy took out her phone from her backpack. "Ugg," she said. "No signal on Mars!"

"I wish we were home on Jupiter," said Tina.

Just then the ground under them started to shake and tremble.

"Goodness!" they shouted as they looked at each other.

A hole in the red soil started to open next to them.

The hole got wider and wider.

Trudy and Tina just had time to grab
each other before they fell through the hole
and were gone.

"Get off me!" said Trudy as she pushed her sister off her back. They had fallen quite far but landed safely on the soft ground.

"We can't get out the way we came," said Tina as she dusted herself off.

"Ms. Bickleblorb said to explore," added Trudy. "So let's explore!"

2 WHO IS THIS?

They had not gone far when they heard someone or something crying.

"Let's go back the way we came," said Tina nervously.

"Nonsense," said Trudy. "Nothing scares me!"

Around the next curve they saw a tiny
creature sobbing.

"Ewwww!" said Tina. "That looks
yucky!"

Trudy went over and gently picked up
the tiny alien. It instantly stopped crying
and smiled at her. The creature licked her
face with its purple tongue.

"Oh isn't he precious?" Trudy said. "I'll name him Spot!"

"You can't keep him!" said Tina.

Trudy ignored her sister. She let Spot ride in her backpack with its head sticking out.

Soon the tunnel ended.

"Rats," said Tina "We are still stuck down here."

They tried other paths, but every tunnel they took ended the same way. There was no way out!

3 WE ARE IN TROUBLE

MUNCH, MUNCH, MUNCH.

A loud munching sound was coming from behind them and getting closer. "What do we do?" cried Tina.

An ugly, green monster with giant teeth was munching its way right toward them.

"*HELP!*" shouted Tina.

Trudy reached into her backpack and pulled out her notebook. She also gave Spot a quick snuggle.

"I think we read about these guys in school," she said.

"*HURRY!*" said Tina. "Before we get eaten!"

Trudy flipped through pages of her book. "Humm, that's not it," she said calmly. "Maybe it was near the end?"

"*WE ARE GOING TO GET SQUISHED!*" shouted Tina, who was frantically trying to climb out of the way. The monster was getting closer.

"Ah, here it is!" said Trudy as she
pointed to a picture in the book.

"It's a Mars Rock Muncher," she said.
"He is quite gentle... unless you are a
rock."

The monster was right at their heels.

"Follow me!" said Trudy. Then she jumped in the air and landed on the monster's back as he passed them by.

"Wait for me!" Tina shouted as she closed her eyes and jumped on too.

The Mars Rock Muncher didn't pay them any attention. But when he got to the end of the tunnel those giant munching teeth started eating a hole right through the rock.

"*Jumping Jupiter!*" shouted Trudy with a laugh. "Hang on!"

They hung on tight as the monster dug
a tunnel left, then right, then down.
Finally he turned and headed straight up!
"Here we go!" said Trudy.

They broke through to the surface
of the planet.

The Jupiter twins hopped off.

Trudy smiled but Tina could barely
stand on her own two legs.

They were just in time to see the space bus with their teacher and fellow students being sucked into the mouth of a giant jelly-like alien.

"That doesn't look good," said Trudy.

Tina nearly fainted.

"There is something familiar about that alien," said Trudy as she reached into her backpack for her notebook again.

Just then, Spot jumped out and started running right toward the alien.

"Blip. Blap. Bloop," he shouted.

Once the giant alien saw Spot, she spit out the space bus.

PITOOEY

"Bloopykins," she roared as she scooped Spot up.

"It's Spot's mother!" said Trudy.
"That's why Spot must have been crying."

The mother alien slid away smiling
with Spot riding on her back.

Trudy looked sad.

Tina put her arm around her sister.
"Spot will be happier now," she said.

Ms. Bickleblorb scraped the alien goo off the bus and waved to the twins.

"Hop aboard girls," she called.

The space bus rocketed off into space, heading back home to Jupiter.

That night Trudy was sad.

"I miss Spot," she said.

Tina gave Trudy a present.

It was a picture she drew of

her sister holding Spot.

Trudy was happy again.

WHEN I GROW UP
SALLY RIDE

BY AnnMarie Anderson

ILLUSTRATED BY Gerald Kelley

Scholastic Inc.

"All adventures, especially into new territory, are scary."

— SALLY RIDE

This unauthorized biography was carefully researched to make sure it's accurate. Although the book is written to sound like Sally Ride is speaking to the reader, these are not her actual statements.

ISBN 978-0-545-60983-8

12 11 10 9 8 7 6 5 4 3 2 1   15 16 17 18 19/0

Printed in the U.S.A.   40

First printing, January 2015

Book design by Marissa Asuncion

GLOSSARY

astrophysics: The scientific study of the structure of stars, planets, and space.

computer science: The study of computers and their uses.

data: Information collected in a place so that it can be studied.

engineers: Those who are specially trained to design and build machines or large structures such as bridges and roads.

experimenting: Scientifically testing or trying something in order to learn something particular.

meteorology: The study of Earth's atmosphere, especially in relation to climate and weather.

navigation: Finding where you are and where you need to go when you travel in a ship, an aircraft, or other vehicle.

physics: The science that explores matter, energy, and motion.

physiology: The science that deals with the function of living things.

scientific method: Collecting information about a problem, and then testing your ideas about it.

TIME LINE

May 26, 1951:
I was born in Los Angeles, California.

1973:
I graduated from Stanford University with degrees in physics and English.

1978:
I was chosen to join NASA, and became part of the astronaut class of 1979.

June 18, 1983:
As a member of the *Challenger* space shuttle crew, I became the youngest American and the first American woman in space.

October 5, 1984:
I flew on the *Challenger* again in another space shuttle mission.

1986:
I cowrote a children's book called *To Space & Back*.

1989:
I became a professor and director of the California Space Institute at the University of California in San Diego.

2001:
I founded a company, Sally Ride Science, to help kids become interested in math and science.

July 23, 2012:
I died of pancreatic cancer.

In 2001, I founded my own company, Sally Ride Science, to encourage children—especially girls—to stay interested in science and math. Sally Ride Science brings science to life for students and teachers around the country through workshops, educational materials, and science festivals. I died on July 23, 2012, from pancreatic cancer at the age of 61. I received many honors and rewards in my life, including induction into the National Women's Hall of Fame, the Astronaut Hall of Fame, and the Aviation Hall of Fame. But my greatest honor was serving as an inspiration to young people around the world.

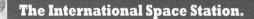

Today, students around the world can request new images be taken from space, and they can also search EarthKam's library of existing photos. Middle-school students also have access to close-up photos of the moon's surface through the MoonKam Project, which I also worked on with NASA.

In 1995, I helped NASA launch a project to enable middle-school students to take photos of Earth using a special camera aboard space shuttle missions. In 2001, EarthKam was permanently installed on the International Space Station.

EarthKam

Photos taken from EarthKam

My love of science had taken me to great heights, and I wanted to pass that joy on to others. So in 1986 I cowrote a children's book called *To Space & Back* to share my amazing experiences in space with others. I went on to write six more books for children about science and space.

The surface of the moon.

After the investigation, I joined NASA's administration and helped plan the space program's future. Then in 1987, I returned to Stanford University for a science fellowship. And in 1989, I became a professor and director of the California Space Institute at the University of California in San Diego. I had returned to my earlier passion—physics research.

The country was shocked. Those astronauts had been my friends and coworkers, and I was deeply saddened by the *Challenger* disaster. President Ronald Reagan formed a committee of thirteen people to investigate the accident and determine what had gone wrong. I was the only astronaut he asked to join.

In June 1985, I was assigned to fly in space a third time. But my training came to a halt when a terrible tragedy occurred. On January 28, 1986, the same shuttle that I had taken to space, *Challenger*, exploded just after takeoff, killing all seven crew members.

I was lucky enough to get a second chance to return to space. On October 5, 1984, I flew on *Challenger* again. It was the thirteenth space shuttle mission. This time, I wasn't the only woman on board—astronaut Kathryn Sullivan was part of the crew, too.

Paul D. Scully-Power.

Robert L. Crippin

Marc Garneau

Jon A. McBride

Me

Kathryn D. Sullivan

David C. Leestma

After we returned to Earth, I received a lot of attention because I had been the first American woman in space. I wished people would focus on the exciting advancements in science that had taken place on the shuttle instead. Still, I came to enjoy being an inspiration to young women and girls around the country.

During our mission, astronaut John Fabian and I successfully used the RMS. We also oversaw science experiments that had been sent into space by companies and schools. But my favorite thing about space was the view of Earth every night before I went to bed. It was incredible!

I spent the next year working closely with the other crew members to prepare for our flight. Finally, on June 18, 1983, I traveled into space on the *Challenger* space shuttle. It was the best day of my life.

Then, in April 1982, my biggest dream came true. I was chosen—along with astronauts Robert Crippen, Frederick Hauck, John Fabian, and Norman Thagard—to fly on the seventh space shuttle flight. At thirty-two years old, I would be the youngest American and the first American woman in space!

I also became NASA's first female capsule communicator, or capcom. The capcom is the only person on Earth who is allowed to talk to the astronauts while they are in space. My work as capcom during the shuttle *Columbia*'s second and third missions proved that I was a team player who could stay calm under pressure.

After a year of training, I became an astronaut. But I still had to be assigned to a space mission, and that could take years. In the meantime, I joined a team of **engineers**. We developed a special fifty-foot-long robotic arm called a remote manipulator system, or RMS, that would be used during missions.

The RMS in action.

U.S. AIR FORCE

U.S. AIR FORCE

Though only some astronauts are pilots, all astronaut candidates had to spend time training in a two-seat T-38 jet. I liked flying so much I eventually went on to earn my pilot's license.

For the next year, the other astronaut classmates and I learned all about the space shuttle. We studied math, **computer science**, **navigation**, **meteorology**, physics, and engineering. I ran every day and lifted weights to keep in shape. And I learned how to parachute during a NASA survival course.

More than 7,000 men and 1,000 women responded to the ad, and I was chosen as one of 208 finalists. After a weeklong interview and months of waiting, I got a phone call from NASA offering me a position in the astronaut class of 1979, along with five other women and twenty-nine men. I was thrilled!

Then one day I was reading the *Stanford Daily* newspaper. An ad from the National Aeronautics and Space Administration (NASA) said they were looking for thirty-five new astronauts. For the first time, women were invited to apply. Suddenly, I knew exactly what job I wanted—to be an astronaut! I sent in my application that day.

The Milky Way galaxy.

I stayed at Stanford for five more years, earning a master's degree in physics and a PhD in **astrophysics**. My research at Stanford involved studying energy given off by stars, but I wasn't sure what type of job I wanted now that I was leaving school as Dr. Sally Ride.

loved my science classes at Stanford. But in my junior year, I took a class about the playwright William Shakespeare. I also loved his plays! When I graduated from Stanford in 1973 I received two degrees—one in **physics** and another in English.

graduated from high school as one of the top six students in my class. Then I took physics classes and played tennis at Swarthmore College in Swarthmore, Pennsylvania, before transferring to Stanford University in Palo Alto, California.

Dr. Mommaerts taught me how to use the **scientific method** to solve problems. I had always loved puzzles, mysteries, and **data**, and now I realized that becoming a scientist would involve all of those things! I had a new dream to pursue.

Thanks to my tennis talent, I received a scholarship to attend a private high school in Los Angeles. In my junior year there, I took a **physiology** class taught by Dr. Elizabeth Mommaerts. That class changed my life.

My love of sports led me to tennis. I practiced hard and was determined to play well. By the time I was twelve, I was competing all across America—and winning! Instead of playing for the Dodgers when I grew up, I now wanted to be a professional tennis player.

When I wasn't reading about sports, I was playing football, softball, or soccer with kids in the neighborhood. I didn't mind being the only girl who wanted to play—I just wanted to win! I learned early in life that it pays to be a team player, and I was usually the first person picked when we chose teams.

I also loved sports. I read the sports pages of the newspaper, especially if there was an article about my favorite baseball team, the Los Angeles Dodgers. I memorized details about the players' ratings and batting averages, and I dreamed that one day I might play baseball for the Dodgers.

I grew up in a cozy home with a lot of books, and I liked to read. My favorite stories were mysteries, spy stories, and science fiction novels. I liked Nancy Drew, James Bond, and Superman. I loved science, too. I spent a lot of time **experimenting** with my chemistry set and telescope.

Los Angeles

Dad

Me

Mom

Karen (Bear)

My name is Sally Kristen Ride. I was born on May 26, 1951, in Los Angeles, California. My dad, Dale, was a college professor, and my mom, Joyce, was a teacher. I had a younger sister named Karen, but I called her Bear because I had trouble saying her name!